Books by Vicki Rickabaugh & Veronica Grace
With illustrations by Vincent Gagliardi, Jr.

The Mysteries of Veron:
The Ruby Realm, 2010

The Mysteries of Veron:
The Carnelian Realm, 2011

Books by Vicki Rickabaugh

Gateway to the Universe:
Knowing Your Inner Self, 2010

Spirits United:
The Sacred Connection, 2010

In the Beauty of the Sunset:
A Spiritual Journey, 2011

The Mysteries of Veron

The Carnelian Realm

By
Vicki Rickabaugh
& Veronica Grace

Illustrations by Vincent Gagliardi, Jr.

Published by Interwoven Connections
Howell, NJ, USA

Printed in the United States.

**Special Thanks to Pamela Turner,
Editor and Graphic Designer.**

Published by
Interwoven Connections
PO Box 686
Howell, NJ 07731
www.interwovenconnectionspubs.com

ISBN-13: 978-0-9829582-4-7

Dedication

To the child who resides within us all,
who sees the world with trust, love and simplicity.
This book is dedicated to my grandchildren —
Ashley, Michael, Nicole and Mya.

To dream, to play in the infinite wonderland,
to fly on the wings of imagination
and know that all things are possible.
This is the vision and the journey.

For my Guardian Angel, who has given me
belief, inner tranquility, stillness and strength.

Even though I will only know your spirit for the moment,
the merging of spirits will be forever.

To Fatima, with gratitude. You have created
music in hearts and souls so that the universe
can hear the symphony.

- Vicki Rickabaugh

Dedication

For My Siblings

Maryann, Joe, Patty, Judy and Eddie

who always supported and encouraged

but never judged the journey

and for

Tara Ann and Kerri Lynn

who made the journey magical

- Veronica Grace

Dedication

To my mother and father, for making me who I am,
for always being there, and supporting me
through good times and in bad.

To my son, Vinnie,
the best accomplishment of my life.
I love you buddy.

Gina, Joe, Eric, Trevor, Heather, Nicole and Joey,
all my love always.

Donna, Carley, and Hannah,
forever in my heart, always on my mind.

And to all my friends, who made this all reality.

- Vincent Gagliardi, Jr.

Meet the Characters

Viva & Eli	An adventurous sister and brother who answer the call of the White Horses and magically travel to the Land of Veron to rescue the village of the Carnelian Realm
Rezza	A Balmurrey from the Ruby Realm
Fern	A Balmurrey from the Carnelian Realm (pronounced "car-kneel-yan")
Sharra	Fern's daughter
Noumbles	A young Carnelian, friend of Sharra
Muskels	Another young Carnelian, friends with Sharra and Noumbles
Dr. Moss	A Carnelian scientist, keeper of the Stream of Nourishment
Merleg	A young Denge bird (pronounced "den-gay")
Mahwah	Leader of the Denge birds, father of Merleg

Contents

Chapter 1
Let's Play Pretend

Eli and Viva were running full speed across the grainy autumn sand, their arms stretched high, holding onto their kites.

They loved this time of year because all the summer people had gone home and they had the boardwalk and the beach all to themselves.

"Let's play pretend," said Eli. "I am a brave knight in shining armor. My kite is a fire-breathing dragon, and I am hunting him down as he flies through the air."

"My hero! I am a princess and my kite is a huge castle with a large wall around it," said Viva. "The dragon is about to attack my castle. You must save me."

The brother and sister loved to have a contest as to whose kite could fly the highest while they ran down the beach.

As the kites flew higher and higher, Eli and Viva began to notice a lot of birds.

But these were not beach birds. They were not white seagulls looking for food. They were large black birds circling the sky as if they were looking for something.

"Those birds don't belong here. Where do you think they came from?" Viva asked Eli.

"I don't know," said Eli. "The winds are really strong today. Maybe they just flew here with the change of weather."

Just then a gust of wind made Eli's kite nose-dive into the sand.

"That's OK, Eli. I was getting tired of flying kites anyway. Want to go up to the boardwalk?"

"Yeah, I hear the ice cream stand is still open."

Viva and Eli rolled up their kite strings and folded up their kites before heading to the boardwalk. "Last one to the steps buys the ice cream." Eli yelled as he started to race towards the edge of the beach.

Together they ran up the stairs, each one trying to nudge the other aside so they could be first.

They both reached the top together and began to laugh so hard they had to sit down.

As they sat catching their breath, they looked ahead towards the seven large white horses on the Merry Go Round, their favorite spot on the boardwalk.

The sun was so bright that the

necklaces on each horse were shining like sparkling jewels. Red ones, green ones, blue ones, a different color for each horse.

"I don't really care about the ice cream," Eli said. "Let's go see the horses."

Eli headed straight for his favorite horse with the fiery red stone at the front of its necklace.

Viva passed up her favorite horse that held the large green stone because she sensed something from the horse that wore the orange stone.

Viva called Eli over and said, "Eli look, the large orange stone is faded and dull. What do you think that could mean?"

Just then the brother and sister heard familiar voices. "Viva, Eli, we're so glad you came back."

Could it be, thought Viva? Were the horses calling to them again?

"You helped us and Rezza in the Ruby Realm against the Grabber Me Alls. Now our friends in the Carnelian Realm need your help very badly. They're almost out of time."

And with a silent knowing between the horses and the children, they were off.

Chapter 2
Trouble for Veron

The Merry Go Round started to spin. It went slowly at first, but then started spinning faster and faster. Finally it was turning so fast that Eli and Viva had to hold on to the horses.

Bump, bump! Eli and Viva hit the ground with a thud. They sat up slowly, thinking they had been thrown off the Merry Go Round.

As they began to look around and saw green grassy hills and red bushes, they realized where they were.

"Uh oh," said Eli, "I think we are

back in the Land of Veron." This made them nervous because they knew from experience that not everyone or everything was friendly in the Land of Veron.

They were sitting in the deep green grass when they heard a rustling in the bushes. They looked at one another with wide eyes as if to ask, "What is that?"

Out from behind one of the bushes came Rezza, their Balmurrey friend from the Ruby Realm. Viva and Eli sprang up like a Jack in the Box and ran to meet Rezza.

"How are you and all the Balmurreys?" Viva asked, as they

were all trading hugs.

"We are OK for now, but we are very scared," Rezza said. "Our friends in the Carnelian Realm are in big trouble. We really need your help."

"Something is attacking the crops, and the animals are starving. Without crops and animals, the Carnelians will soon get very sick. The Realm is dying and could be lost forever."

"That's horrible!" said Eli. "What happened?"

"We don't know exactly," said Rezza sadly.

Just then, another Balmurrey crawled out from behind the bush.

"Oh, Fern. I'm glad you got here safely," said Rezza. "These are my friends Viva and Eli. The white horses sent them here to help us."

"Thank you, oh, thank you so much for coming. We need all the help we can get," said Fern as he squeezed their hands with both of his.

Fern was a little person who stood about three feet tall, the same size as Rezza, but a little different. Instead of being Ruby Red, Fern was a reddish-orange color, with hair to match, looking sort of like an overly ripe peach.

"We'll do whatever we can," said Viva, "but we don't quite understand the problem." Eli nodded in agreement.

Fern began to explain. "In the Carnelian Realm our energy stone sits in the middle of the Stream of Nourishment. Like all Balmurreys, the Carnelians recharge their energy with that stone."

"The stone also energizes the water in the stream. That water is used by all the Carnelians and their animals, and helps all the plants grow healthy."

"Now thousands of birds have moved to the Stream of Nourishment and circle over the stream every day. Each bird stands as tall as an adult Carnelian. When these huge black birds spread their wings, it's as if they could grab hold of four Carnelians at the same time!"

"The flock of birds has grown so large that they nearly block all the sun from recharging the Carnelian Stone."

"Our water used to be crystal clear and our stone used to glow like the brightest sunny day. But without sunlight the water has become cloudy and the stone is dull, almost lifeless."

"Soon we may not be able to survive at all."

"What can we do?" Viva asked. "It all sounds so awful!"

"Only by working together can we figure out a solution," said Rezza. We just can't do it alone."

Chapter 3
More Help Arrives

As Viva and Eli thought about all they had just been told, they were joined by three more Carnelians. The three newcomers all had the same tuft of reddish orange hair, and they were jabbering away all at once.

"The birds have taken over..." "...need your help..." "...stone is dying..." "...not enough food..."

Fern turned to them and said, "Ssshhhhh, one at a time." The three Carnelians looked down at the ground as if to say they were sorry.

"My apologies. They are very worried and feeling afraid," said Fern. "Eli, Viva, these are my friends, Noumbles and Muskels."

"And this is my daughter, Sharra," sighed Fern. "Even though she is young, she insisted upon coming to help."

"We're all working together to help the Carnelian Stone get its energy back," said Noumbles. "We have to hurry before the Denge birds ruin everything."

"They're big and scary, too!" interrupted Muskels. "All day long they flap their wings back and forth over the stream. They eat the plants that grow near the stream and chase away any of our farmers who try to come for food."

"So far the Denges have let us get to the stone to recharge our energy, but they watch every step we take," said Noumbles. "They want to make sure we don't go in the water or come near the plants."

"Because the Denges block the sun, our stone is getting weaker every day," Fern stated, "and it's taking longer for our people to fully recharge their energy."

"Father says that soon we will have to limit each person's time at the stone," added Sharra.

"Then our people will start getting sick."

All of a sudden a big gust of wind blew through the group, knocking Sharra and Viva to the ground.

"Auk, Auk, Auk!" screamed the Denge birds.

"Sharra, Viva, are you OK?" shouted Fern.

"Yes, father. Just a little dusty," answered Sharra, brushing herself off.

"The Denges haven't hurt anyone yet. They just try to keep us away from the stream."

"Wow, they're huge!" said Eli, helping his sister stand up. "I'm not sure what we can do. We don't know anything about birds."

"But, Eli, we've got to do something," replied Viva. "For Rezza. For all the Balmurreys."

Rezza then spoke to Eli and Viva.

"Thank you, my friends, for coming. The Carnelians are good people, and the Denges are really good birds. It's just that something has happened to upset the balance of nature in the Carnelian Realm."

Could these be the same birds

that Eli and I saw on the beach at home, Viva thought to herself. Was that a message for us?

With a sadness in her voice, Viva quietly started to sing.

Release Old and Young,
Give Balance in Veron.

Hearing the familiar song, the others soon joined her, singing together for success in the mission that was ahead.

"Good luck to you all," said Rezza." I must return home now, but the Balmurreys in the Ruby Realm will only be a holler away if you need us," added Rezza as he waved goodbye to his friends.

Chapter 4
Into the Woods

As Rezza walked away towards home, Eli, Viva and the Carnelian Balmurreys continued to talk about the problem with the Denge birds.

"Isn't there anyone in the Carnelian Realm who knows about birds?" asked Eli. "What about a veterinarian?" "Or an animal trainer?" added Viva.

"We have somebody better than that. He knows just about everything about animals and nature. His name is Dr. Pete Moss," said Noumbles.

"He is our best scientist!" bragged Muskels. "He is the Keeper of the Stream of Nourishment."

Fern went on. "Dr. Moss discovered the problem with the stream. He knows that the Denge birds have changed the balance in the Carnelian Realm, but he doesn't know how to fix it."

"We should go see him," said Eli. "Maybe together we can start to figure something out."

Viva, Eli, Fern and the other Balmurreys started their climb on the path up the steep hill toward Dr. Moss' cabin.

As they climbed, Viva noticed that the sky was becoming darker. It confused her because it was still early afternoon.

She could barely see the houses of the village as they passed. If it wasn't for the voices of the Carnelians talking as they went about their daily chores, Viva wouldn't have been sure there even was a village.

"We are coming to a bridge over the Stream of Nourishment," Fern told them. "Dr. Moss' house is just up the road."

As they crossed the stream, Eli looked at the huge oak trees all around. He noticed that the trees were stripped almost bare of their leaves and had no acorns.

The tree limbs reached high into the air. When the wind blew the ends of the bare branches looked like the boney fingers of some terrible creature reaching out, nearly grabbing the visitors.

Viva saw that the trees were filled with huge black birds. Because they were so large, she wondered how the trees were able to hold all that weight.

There were so many birds that hardly any sunlight could shine through the trees.

The Denges sat very still as

everyone passed, but the birds never took their eyes off them.

Fern saw the scared look on the faces of Viva and Eli. "Sometimes the Denges just sit and stare at us, but they've never hurt us yet."

Viva could see a small log cabin ahead along the path. It had no windows, just little slits every so often in between the logs to let in some light.

There were twisted vines growing in every direction all over the cabin and hanging over the door. Surely no one had lived in this house for a very long time.

As they got closer to the cabin, the front door swung open wide. There stood Dr. Peter Moss, keeper of the Stream of Nourishment.

"I thought I heard voices outside. Welcome to my home," said Dr. Moss.

Dr. Moss was about four feet tall, just a little taller than the other Carnelians. He had orange wiry hair that stood straight up on his head and went in all directions. He wore large orange rimmed eyeglasses that sat on a round nose.

Viva and Eli heard the birds in the nearby trees screech as they saw

Dr. Moss. Fern and the other Balmurreys looked worried.

Wonder what that's all about, Viva thought as they entered the cabin.

Chapter 5
A Meeting With Dr. Moss

The inside of Dr. Moss' house looked almost as wild as the outside. There were overflowing bookshelves on every wall, and there were stacks of papers on every piece of furniture.

"Please do come in. I'm sorry for the mess, but it's just that I've been working so hard to figure out this problem," said Dr. Moss, as he ran around the room grabbing papers and clearing off places for his guests to sit down.

After exchanging greetings, everyone found seats around the

big oak table that Dr. Moss had cleared off.

Dr. Moss stood in the center of the room and began to pace back and forth. Viva and Eli waited for him to speak.

"I just don't know what to do anymore," he said, continuing to pace. "The whole situation is very bad, very bad. I'm so glad you've come. I've tried everything. I'm at my wits end." Dr. Moss continued walking in circles and pulling at his hair.

"The Denge birds used to live throughout the Carnelian Realm. We all used to live here in harmony," continued Dr. Moss.

"Then something happened. They all started living very near the Stream of Nourishment in the oak trees and started feeding on the plants near the stream."

"Now the Denges have become so destructive that our whole environment is in trouble. We need to find a way to bring the balance back."

"Come, it's easier to explain if I show you," said Dr. Moss as he motioned for Viva and Eli to follow him back outside.

The group did not go back on the path but followed Dr. Moss directly into the woods towards the Stream of Nourishment.

As they got close to the stream, Eli could see a large orange stone, way too big to move, sitting in the middle of the water. It looked to Eli like six people could stand on it easily, but it's color was very dull.

On one side of the stone, Eli could see a path of smaller stones. They led from the edge of the stream, right across the water, straight up to the Carnelian Stone.

Dr. Moss saw what Eli was looking at and explained. "Those are stepping stones. We use them to walk across the water to the back of the Carnelian Stone."

"We climb the steps on the back of the Stone. Once on top, we plug ourselves into the Stone and recharge our energy centers.

"Like all the Balmurreys in Veron, we have slits in our feet to connect to the Stone," said Dr. Moss, lifting his foot up to show the slit.

Dr. Moss, Viva and Eli passed the stone and walked a little further downstream. Viva looked up in the trees and saw the Denges begin to stir as the group of visitors walked underneath. She trembled as she remembered her close call with the Denges when she first met Sharra.

Dr. Moss spoke to his visitors. "The Denge birds are large and powerful. They eat almost any type of plant life. And when they fly together, the wind created by their huge wings is strong enough to blow us down to the ground."

"Oh, yes, we know," said Viva and Sharra, nodding in agreement.

"This area by the Carnelian Stone is where the problem is the worst. Because there are so many birds now, it is like a dark blanket covering the sun.

"If our stone does not get sunlight, it cannot nourish the stream and provide food. If we do not find a way to solve this problem soon, no one in the Carnelian Realm will be able to survive."

Viva sat down by the stream and found herself wishing for a magic wand or at the very least a Fairy God Mother. Not knowing what else to do, she started to sing very quietly.

Release Old and Young
Give Balance In Veron

Chapter 6
The Garden of Willbedone

Eli moved closer and sat beside Viva. He put his arm around her shoulder to offer her comfort and support. "What do you think we can do? How can we find out what is causing the Denges to act this way?"

Viva dropped her head and was about to tell Eli she had no idea what they could do when Sharra came along.

With her sweet smile and yellow hair ribbons flowing over her shoulders, she looked like a ray of sunshine on a cloudy day. Sharra knelt beside Viva and spoke in a soft voice. "Come, come with me. The others have already gone ahead."

Viva and Eli stood up and followed Sharra. They weren't sure why, but they didn't know what else to do.

They walked along the winding path of the forest, being careful not to get caught on the thorny bushes or hit their heads on the low hanging branches.

Suddenly, Viva recognized where she was. "We are going to the Garden of Willbedone. I remember the Garden from the Ruby Realm."

Sure enough, after another minute Viva started hearing the familiar soft singing, and soon Sharra led them into the circle of the Garden.

There, sitting in the circle were several Balmurreys from the Carnelian realm including Muskels and Noumbles. With them were several young Denge birds. They were all singing together:

Release Old and Young
Give Balance in Veron

Eli and Viva were shocked to see Carnelians and Denges sitting so peacefully together. After all, Dr. Moss had told them that the birds were causing all the problems.

Eli went up to Noumbles and asked, "Why are the Denges here in the Garden of Willbedone?

Noumbles introduced Eli and Viva to one of the young Denges. "My name is Merleg," he said. "Please, sit with us. I want to tell you a story."

"The Carnelian Realm used to be a beautiful place where everyone got along peacefully," started Merleg. "Then our parents got upset with the Carnelians and made us all move close to the stream."

"We don't know why, but nobody trusts each other anymore."

Off in the distance Viva and Eli could hear the screech of the Denges that were still hanging over the Stream of Nourishment. They could tell by the loud sound of their auk, auk, auk that they were getting restless.

Suddenly there was a rustling in the thorny bushes to the left of the Garden. Viva and Eli watched, their eyes wide with surprise as Dr. Moss came stumbling out of the bushes.

"Oh good," he said, "I see Sharra has gotten both of you here.

Good work, Sharra!" Fern was right behind Dr. Moss.

Dr. Moss motioned for all of them to come to the center of the circle.

The scientist began, "We are here to discover what has made the Denge birds upset and distrustful and put the Carnelian Realm out of balance."

"This is a mystery to us as the name Denge actually means balance. We must find out what has happened so we can bring balance back for us all."

As Dr. Moss finished, everyone in the Garden heard a crashing noise up in the air near the stream. They all turned towards the sound.

Two male Denges seemed to be attacking one another. Their wings were spread wide, the claws on their feet extended like sharp knives, and their feathers flying like a torn pillow in a pillow fight.

Dr. Moss gathered the children close to him and said, "This is not good, this is not good at all."

As Viva watched she noticed the birds never left the area where they were fighting. She noticed they did not try to fly away from one another.

Viva told Dr. Moss that they should wait until night fall and then try to see what was in the trees that the Denges were fighting over.

Chapter 7
Exploring at Night

As the sun set and darkness fell over the forest, Viva sat listening to the chirp of the crickets.

Soon it was time to leave. Together Viva, Eli, Dr. Moss, Fern and Sharra made their way to the tree where the Denges had their battle. The half moon gave them just enough light to see the path.

Noumbles, Muskels and some of the others followed but stayed at a distance behind. The young Denges stayed back in the Garden for now.

Everyone in the group started

looking up in the tree to see what might have caused the birds to begin their loud fight.

In the pale moonlight, Eli was the first to spy it. "Look, on that branch on the left. I think it's a nest."

"Why, Eli, I think you're right," said Dr. Moss. "That's just the kind of nest that Denges make."

The scientist was excited to investigate the size of the nest and see how it was made.

"I wonder if there are any eggs in the nest?" questioned Sharra. Just then, the visitors started to hear a soft chirping sound.

As they looked up, a female Denge brought food to the nest.

"I guess the eggs have already hatched," added Viva excitedly.

"Maybe I should climb up and take a look," said Dr. Moss, as he reached for the lowest limb.

Just then a pair of huge male Denges appeared out of nowhere, knocking Dr. Moss off his feet. They were gone as fast as they came.

Dr. Moss was startled, but not hurt. "I guess they don't want anyone… (cough, cough)… messing with their nest," he

whispered, as he tried to catch his breath.

Viva asked aloud, "Has anyone ever checked out the Stream of Nourishment to see why the Denges have all moved there?"

Muskels answered, "A few of us went downstream with Dr. Moss, but we could only go so far."

"The Denges started to squawk loudly and swoop down on us and wouldn't let us go any further," added Noumbles.

"Wait a minute," said Eli suddenly. "Something's not right."

"When we first arrived in the Carnelian Realm, we saw the Denges, but they didn't do anything. They just looked at us.

"When we came to the Garden of Willbedone with the young Carnelians and the young Denges, the adult birds did not bother us.

"Since we've been here, the only time the birds started to fly at us or make loud noises was when Dr. Moss or other adult Carnelians were around.

"It is as if the Denges want to protect all young living things.

"Sir, I mean no disrespect, but perhaps Viva and I and some of the other children, both Carnelians and Denges, could explore the Stream of Nourishment. Perhaps the adult birds will let us pass by."

Dr. Moss pondered Eli's plan and then turned to Fern. "Perhaps the boy is right, Fern. We've tried everything, without success. Maybe the children can have more luck than we did."

Fern looked worried, but finally agreed. "Let's go back to the Garden and sleep. Then the children can make a fresh start in the daylight."

Back at the Garden of Willbedone those who had stayed behind had already started a fire and made up sleeping areas for the night.

Before ending their day, the group gathered once more singing softly all together:

Release Old and Young
Give Balance in Veron

Chapter 8
Children Venture Alone

When Fern woke up the next morning, the children were already up, excited to explore the Stream of Nourishment.

Viva told Fern, "We're going to split into two groups so we can search on both sides of the stream at once."

"Just be careful," warned Fern. "The Denges are everywhere, and we really don't know exactly how dangerous they can be."

"I think we'll be safe as long as the young Denges are with us," added Eli. "Come, friends. We need to get going."

The children walked down to the stream by the Carnelian Stone. Merleg and Eli led a team of Carnelians and Denges across the stepping stones to the other side of the stream. Sharra and Viva led the team on the close side of the stream.

Both groups started downstream looking for anything that might explain the Denges' changed behavior.

As the children continued walking downstream, the adult Denges stared in silence high in the trees.

Viva noticed that a few birds flew above them as they continued on their journey. The birds kept their distance, but they never took their eyes off the children.

"This is as far as Dr. Moss got," said Sharra. "The birds started swooping down and cackling loudly and wouldn't let him go any farther."

"The birds aren't bothering us now," said Eli. "Let's keep going."

The groups on both sides of the stream continued moving ahead, being careful to avoid thorny bushes and tree roots.

"Stop!!" shouted Viva suddenly.

Everyone turned to see what Viva was looking at.

There, in the middle of the stream, a short distance ahead, was a fallen tree. A giant tree, with its branches going in every direction, completely blocked the path of the stream and stopped the flow of water!

"Quick, down here." The young Denge Merleg had flown beyond the tree trunk and was calling to the others for help.

Sharra came running. Tangled in a clump of branches in the fallen tree she could just barely see a nest of Denge babies.

From where he circled, Merleg saw ten or more baby Denges that were very sickly.

They could hardly move and were whimpering. Their tiny bodies were little balls of soft gray fur that were bare in spots. They didn't even look up at Merleg, as though it were too much of an effort to move their heads.

Merleg and Sharra told Viva, Eli and the others what they had seen.

"So that's it"! Viva shouted. "They are trying to save their babies!!"

"Because the tree blocked the stream, the Denges must have moved up near the Carnelian Stone to help their babies survive," continued Viva excitedly.

"We need to move this tree so that the Stream of Nourishment can flow freely," announced Eli.

"But we aren't strong enough. We must bring more help. Then maybe Dr. Moss can help the babies."

Viva spoke to Merleg and the young Denges in their group.

"Go, talk to your parents. The Carnelians can move the tree, but the Denges must allow them to do the work. If we work together, we can all live in peace and survive."

Chapter 9
How to Save the Babies

Viva took Eli by the arm and moved him away from the others.

"Eli, look at the angle of the tree. That top branch must be 40 feet up in the air. Before we can move the tree, we will have to take the babies out of the nest. Otherwise they will fall in the stream when we move the tree."

Eli looked at the fallen tree lying in the water and realized that Viva was right. If they tried to move the tree before saving the babies, the babies would fall into the stream and drown. They weren't strong enough to survive that kind of fall.

Viva and Eli returned to the stream and explained the situation to the others.

"The tree trunk is very slippery and slimy," said Muskels, one of the young Carnelians. "I don't know how you are going to be able to get to the babies without falling yourself."

Eli stood at the base of the fallen tree trunk and took a deep breath. "I just have to try to do this," he thought.

Eli knelt down and wrapped his arms around the trunk. He could feel the slime. It felt like jelly slipping through his fingers.

He inched up the trunk very slowly, ducking under or grabbing onto limbs that were spreading out everywhere on the sides of the trunk – big ones, small ones, sharp ones that were poking at him.

Viva, Sharra, Muskels and the others were standing on the edge of the stream. They were all holding their breath. Sharra had her eyes covered. They were very scared for Eli. What if he fell in the stream?

Eli slowly put one hand in front of the other and slid his body up the

trunk. He had to go very slowly because he could feel himself slipping from side to side as he moved.

Viva let out a gasp and grabbed Muskels arm. It looked as though Eli was going to fall, but he quickly grabbed a branch and righted himself on the trunk.

Eli finally reached the nest. He then realized he couldn't bring all the babies back at once, and he didn't think he would be able to make this trip nine more times.

How was he going to save the Denge babies? How could he get them and himself back to the edge of the stream safely?

Eli held onto the tree trunk trying to come up with an idea and trying harder not to let everyone else see how scared he really was.

Chapter 10
A Surprising Rescue Team

As he held onto the trunk thinking, Eli heard the adult Carnelians and Denge birds coming toward the Stream of Nourishment.

The Carnelians were running and the Denges were flying in formation directly overhead. Surprisingly, they seemed to be traveling together, with the same goal.

Dr. Moss, who had already arrived, was standing on the edge of the stream by the fallen tree.

He knew, but didn't tell anyone, that not only were the baby Denges trapped out there, but so was Eli. "What to do," he thought, "what to do."

When the adult Denges and Carnelians arrived, a Denge approached Fern very calmly, with his head bent down as a sign of peace.

"My name is Mahwah. I am the leader of these Denges. Our children told us how your children have been trying to help our babies, and I want to say Thank You."

"The tree fell onto the stream many months ago. It blocked the flow of water but our babies were alright at first. So we moved upstream for food and continued to fly back to the tree to feed the birds in the nest."

"Then just a few weeks ago, during a storm, the strong winds blew the branches of the tree in all directions, and our nest fell deeper into the tangled mess."

"We are very large birds and could no longer reach our babies to feed them. We were afraid that the Carnelians might find our nest, so we had to scare you away to protect the babies at all costs."

"Now our babies are very sick.

Your children have been very kind to us, and showed us that we were wrong to mistrust the Carnelians. We want to help, as well."

Fern welcomed Mahwah and the adult Denges. "Thank you."

"Based on what the children have explained to us, we have come up with an idea," added Mahwah. "If we all work together we can save everyone."

Fern said at this point he was willing to listen to any ideas.

After talking together, Fern and Mahwah walked back to the edge of the stream. The adult Denge yelled to Eli to get ready to lift the babies one by one into the air. Eli heard the instructions but while he was hanging on for dear life, he was busy watching below.

Fern was lining up all the adult Carnelians along the edge of the stream and telling them to lie down on their bellies.

"What could this be?" Eli was thinking. "How is this going to save us?"

Eli saw ten adult Denge birds stand on the backs of the ten Carnelians who were lying on the ground.

All of a sudden the first Denge

lifted a Carnelian into the air with him. His claws were hooked into the belt loops of the Carnelian's pants.

Eli immediately understood now what was going to happen. He carefully slid up the trunk toward the nest. Then he reached deep into the tangle of branches and carefully took one baby out of the nest.

When the first Denge bird and Carnelian reached him, Eli handed up the first baby bird into the hands of the Carnelian. The pair flew back to edge of the stream and Dr. Moss put the baby into a basket.

As soon as the first pair was back on the ground the second pair flew off. Again Eli handed a baby up to the Carnelian, and continued to do so until all ten babies were safely with Dr. Moss.

Mahwah made one more trip back to the tree. "Now it's your turn, Eli. You've been very brave, but it's time to get you down."

"Just turn your back towards me and I'll grab your belt." Soon Eli was lifted off the tree. His rescuer first soared safely up and away from the tree before gently bringing Eli to the shore.

"Wow, this is a great trip." thought Eli. "Birds are sure lucky.

They get to do this all the time!"

Everyone was standing and clapping for Eli when his feet hit the ground. Viva ran over to hug him. As she did she got slime all over herself. She didn't care, though, because she was just so happy that Eli was safely back.

Chapter 11
Caring for the Babies

The Carnelians and the Denges now wanted to start removing the tree from the stream. However, Dr. Moss said first they had to take care of the babies, and told everyone to follow him to the Garden of WillBeDone.

As they approached the Garden they could hear the soft singing.

Release Old and Young
Give Balance in Veron

Once in the Garden, Dr. Moss led the adult Denges to the Baobab trees that grew in a grove on one side of the Garden. Dr. Moss explained to the birds that the Baobab tree is called the Tree of Life because it contains so many vitamins and other healthy ingredients.

"The fruit, also called Monkey's Bread, contains more Vitamin C than at least three oranges, and the leaves and seeds have more calcium than milk."

"Also, the trunk of the Baobab can hold gallons and gallons of fresh water that we can give to the babies to drink."

"No wonder it's called the Tree of Life," said one of the Denge.

Together, the Denges and Carnelians began gathering the fruit, seeds, leaves and water which Dr. Moss mashed into a paste that could be fed to the babies.

Everyone took turns through the night feeding the babies. The mother Denge birds even let Eli and Viva feed their babies because they knew their new friends were safe and kind.

Mahwah walked over to Fern who was sitting in the circle of WillBeDone. "May I sit with you?" Fern nodded.

As he sat down beside Fern, Mahwah continued, "I want to

thank you for all your help and for the help of all the Carnelians in saving our babies."

Fern said, "I just wish we had known sooner what the problem was. We could have helped sooner."

Mahwah said, "I know that now, but we were afraid to ask for help. We were afraid for our babies. Next time there is a problem, we will know we all have to work together to solve it."

Fern put his arm around Mahwah, barely able to reach to the middle of the large bird's back, feeling the strong bones in his feathers as he did. "Then today was a very good day," Fern said. "In the morning, after we have all rested, we will return to the stream and remove the tree. For tonight we will all sit in the circle in the Garden of WillBeDone together.

Soon many new voices were heard singing:

> Release Old and Young
> Give Balance in Veron

Chapter 12
Balance in Veron

The young friends, Noumbles, Merleg and Muskels, were up first early the next morning. They walked around the Garden waking everyone, telling them it was time to get started on the job of moving the tree from the Stream.

The Carnelians and the Denges walked together toward the stream. Dr. Moss stayed behind with the mother Denges to care for the babies, who were now starting to feel better.

When they arrived at the stream Fern and Mahwah separated everyone into three teams. Viva and Eli each led a team of Carnelians on the ground, while Merleg led a team of Denges in the air.

Now that the baby Denges were out of the tree they were able to tie several ropes around the trunk. Viva, Eli and their two teams pulled the tree from ground level, while the Denges flew with ropes in their mouths, pulling the tree from the air.

Together they tugged and dragged the tree. The Denges flapped their wings as hard as they could, while the Carnelians

were slipping on the wet ground until finally, together, they were able to pull the tree out of the water.

When they got the last branches up onto the ground they heard a roaring, gushing sound. The stream had once again begun to flow.

Viva felt something very warm on her back. When she looked up she saw there weren't any birds in the trees, so the sun was able to shine brightly all around.

Viva saw everyone standing and staring up stream. At first she didn't know what they were looking at. Then she saw it, a bright orange glow slowly filling the sky. The Carnelian stone was getting its energy back from the sun!

The Denges and the Carnelians were all hugging each other and congratulating each other on what a good job they had done together.

Then one by one Fern started leading the older Carnelians to the stone so they could "plug in" and recharge their energy.

Eli and Viva saw Dr. Moss walking toward the stream. She couldn't be sure but Viva thought she saw tears in Dr. Moss's eyes.

"I'm just so happy the Stream of Nourishment is flowing again," he said. "We can't thank you enough."

After a while, all the Carnelians and Denges had returned to the Garden of WillBeDone, all except for Dr. Moss, Fern and Sharra.

"They have all gone to give thanks that we now have our Stream of Nourishment flowing once more and that balance has been returned to Veron," said Dr. Moss.

When he spoke those words, everyone knew it was time for Viva and Eli to return home. Dr. Moss, Fern and Sharra led Viva and Eli back down the path toward the Ruby Realm.

As they got closer to the bushes where they had first met Fern Eli said, "We're glad we could help the Carnelians and the Denges." Viva added, "We'll be back if you ever need us again."

Soon Eli and Viva began to feel as though they were spinning, spinning round and round very fast. Eli held on tight to Viva's hand.

When the spinning stopped, he opened his eyes and saw they were back with the seven magnificent white horses on the merry-go-round.

"Oh, look, Viva, look," Eli shouted as he ran toward the horse with the orange reddish stone. The stone was no longer dull, but shining as brightly as the ruby red stone.

"We did it, we did it," Eli shouted. "We helped the Balmurreys in the Carnelian Realm."

Viva was also excited as she looked at the two shining stones. Then she looked at the stones on the other five horses.

She noticed that the large yellow stone hanging from the neck of the horse next to her was very pale with almost no color at all.

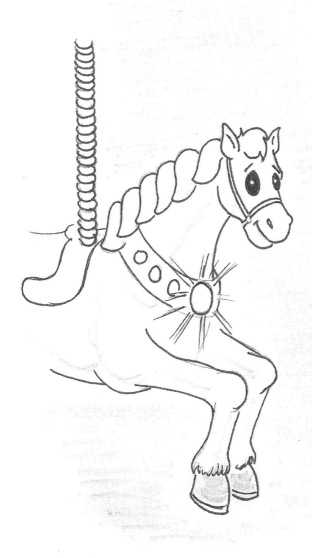

"Eli, I wonder how long it will be before we are needed again in the Land of Veron."

They walked together along the boardwalk trying to decide whether or not they should get that ice cream cone before they returned home. As they walked along they sang to each other:

Release Old and Young
Give balance In Veron

Watch for the next
exciting adventure with
Viva and Eli
in the further

Mysteries of Veron

The Mysteries of Veron

An exciting series for young readers

Written by Vicki Rickabaugh & Veronica Grace
With illustrations by Vincent Gagliardi, Jr.

Seven magnificent white horses share adventures with Viva and Eli in *The Mysteries of Veron*. In Volume 1, join Viva and Eli as they follow the call of the white horses and magically travel to the land of Veron to save the village of *The Ruby Realm*. In Volume 2, Viva and Eli return to Veron to solve a mystery in *The Carnelian Realm.*

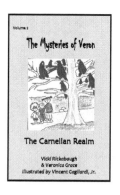

Volume 1
The Ruby Realm
ISBN: 978-0-9829582-2-3

Volume 2
The Carnelian Realm
ISBN: 978-0-9829582-4-7

Published by Interwoven Connections
PO Box 686, Howell, NJ 07731
www.interwovenconnectionspubs.com

Additional Writings by Vicki Rickabaugh

Gateway to the Universe: Knowing Your Inner Self

With photography by
Pamela Turner

ISBN: 978-0-9829582-0-9

Spirits United: The Sacred Connection

With photography by
Pamela Turner

ISBN: 978-0-9829582-1-6

In the Beauty of the Sunset: A Spiritual Journey

With photography by
Pamela Turner

ISBN: 978-0-9829582-3-0

Published by Interwoven Connections
PO Box 686, Howell, NJ 07731
www.interwovenconnectionspubs.com